J   Krensky

Dragon Circle

THE
DRAGON
CIRCLE

Stephen Krensky

Aladdin Books
Macmillan Publishing Company
New York

For my parents

First Aladdin Books edition 1990

Aladdin Books
Macmillan Publishing Company
866 Third Avenue, New York, NY 10022
Collier Macmillan Canada, Inc.

Printed in the United States of America

10 9 8 7 6 5 4 3 2

Library of Congress Cataloging-in-Publication Data

Krensky, Stephen.
    The dragon circle / Stephen Krensky.—1st Aladdin Books ed.
        p. cm.
    Summary: The magical Wynd family becomes involved with dragons
needing help in recovering treasure lost centuries before at the
bottom of a lake. Sequel: *The Witching Hour.*
    ISBN 0-689-71365-7
    [1. Magic—Fiction. 2. Dragons—Fiction.] I. Title
PZ7.K883Dr 1990
[Fic]—dc20   89-29603
                                                        CIP
                                                        AC

ONE

THE HOUSE was in an uproar. A very angry Jennifer Wynd was chasing her younger brother, Perry, around the living room. She was terribly quick, but then so was Perry, prompted by the little balls of fire Jennifer was throwing at his heels.

Fireballs were Jennifer's specialty, something Perry had forgotten earlier when he pulled her long blond hair and shouted, "Alll abooaaarrrd." Perry, of course, had his own specialties, but matching his nine years of experience against Jennifer's twelve was an uphill struggle. After all, though the Wynds were taught magic at an early age, a three-year lead was a distinct advantage.

Magic was a Wynd family tradition, practiced for countless generations, most recently in the village of Westbridge, Massachusetts. It was, however, a secret tradition; even in the twentieth century, the thought of the Salem witch trials was never too far away.

Before long, Jennifer and Perry attracted a spectator—their older sister, Alison. Since Mrs. Wynd was visiting in Boston for the week, and Professor Wynd was reading in his study, Alison had decided to take charge. At sixteen, she considered taking charge her prerogative.

"All right, you two, that's enough now. Stop trampling down the house."

Perry wanted to oblige her, but he was too busy ducking fireballs. Jennifer never had cared much for Alison's prerogatives.

"Really, children!" said Alison.

The battle went on.

"So be it," she murmured, pointing a finger at them both.

Perry and Jennifer suddenly froze. The fireball poised in Jennifer's hand flickered and went out. "You're such a busybody, Alison," she fumed. "Perry and I were just having a little discussion, that's all." With a determined effort, she squirmed loose from the holding spell and darted to her room.

Alison released Perry. "Some discussion," he said, wrinkling his nose at his charred sneakers. "Jenny is too good a shot. But someday . . ."

"Someday you'll get what you deserve," said Alison. "Don't waste that innocent look on me. Now go away, and for your own sake, stay out of Jenny's way."

Perry wandered outside into the bright May sunshine. He surveyed the four ancient oak trees that stood like quiet sentinels around the house. With a nautical air, he climbed into the largest of them, a midshipman ordered by his captain to watch for pirates from the mizzen top of a clipper ship. "We need a young pair of eyes today, Mr. Wynd, so watch sharply." Midshipman Wynd looked out over the Berkshire Mountains, scanning the waves of hills for an enemy vessel. And lo! What did he see off the starboard bough? Well, not pirates exactly, but his two brothers, Edward and Jamie, returning from a walk in the forest.

Perry scuttled to the ground, the pirates all but forgotten in his eagerness to test a new spell.

Edward and Jamie were both laughing heartily as they reached the garden. They didn't really look like brothers—fourteen-year-old Edward was tall and slender like their father; Jamie, a year younger, was a bit short and more than a bit stout. Then, too, Jamie's laugh set them apart. It resembled the roar of the charging water buffalo, at least Perry thought so as he listened.

Suddenly, Edward grabbed Jamie's arm. "Look there by the stone wall!" he exclaimed.

Jamie looked. "What about it?" he asked.

"Don't you see something peculiar?"

"Ground fog, maybe."

"This late in the day? It would have burned off already." Edward peered closely at the wavering mist. "Look again," he said.

Jamie squinted in the sunlight. "Well, well, well," he cried. "A good try, Perry, but you'll have to do better than that to escape Nancy Abbott."

Perry sighed and blinked into sight. Jamie would have to remind him of his misery—the school play about Camelot. Perry had the part of King Arthur, and Nancy Abbott played Queen Guinevere. Perry thought she was a royal pain, and he made no secret about it. He had wanted to be Merlin, but his teacher, Mrs. Hartwick, hadn't thought he looked the part. A lot she knew.

"You did fool me at first," Jamie admitted. "That counts for something."

"Cheer up, Perry," said Edward. "You'll be a new man after lunch. Do you know if it's ready yet? I'm starved."

Jamie laughed. "After the muddle you made of breakfast, we're all starved. Luckily, lunch is in more capable hands. It's Alison's turn, I think." He grinned. "Tell you what, Perry. Why not try your spell on her? We'll help you, right, Edward?"

"Of course."

Perry smiled broadly. A chance like this was not to be passed up.

Shortly thereafter, an invisible Perry entered the house and stood silently by the kitchen door. Alison walked past him into the dining room, carrying a tray of sandwiches. She didn't even blink.

"AHHAAA!!!" shouted Perry, popping into sight.

Alison jumped about a foot, dropping the tray as she whirled about in surprise. Fortunately, only the tray itself fell to the floor, the sandwiches floated unharmed in the air. Edward and Jamie had seen to that. They were too hungry to spoil lunch, even for the sake of a good joke.

"Why, you little imp, Perry!" stormed Alison. "You scamp! I could just strangle you. But I don't see how . . ."

Behind her, Edward and Jamie snickered loudly. Alison turned. "I might have known you two would be involved," she said. "It would have served you right to go hungry."

Edward stepped forward. "Forgive us, Alison," he pleaded solemnly. "It was a mad, impetuous idea."

"Never mind the big words, just put the sandwiches on the table. Then go wash up for lunch. Honestly," she muttered, marching back to the kitchen, "there are more little children in this family than I thought."

A few minutes later, the call for lunch echoed around the house. Some minutes after that, Professor Wynd looked up from the scattered papers on his desk, ran a hand through his rumpled hair, and rose to leave the room. He could not be called a handsome man, but there was a distinguished look to his long, angular face and penetrating blue eyes. And beneath his settled scholarly air lurked a mischievous spirit, which popped to the surface at unexpected moments.

Alison smiled as he entered the dining room. "We had to call you four times, Father. You shouldn't work so hard."

"You mean follow the example of my children?"

"You know exactly what I mean."

The Professor sighed. "I suppose I do. I hope you know, Alison, that you sound more like your mother every day. Perhaps you're right, though. If I can find some company, I'll go for a walk this afternoon."

The company was no problem; everyone wanted to go. The most interesting things happened on walks with Father.

An hour later the whole family was wandering over the hillsides, fording the streams, and straddling the gullies that came their way.

At one point, the Professor strolled absently down a rocky trail, his hands buried deep in his pockets. Looking up, he stared vacantly at a cluster of wildflowers. Then after a moment, he called to the children.

When everyone had gathered round, he said, "I thought we might have a contest."

"A contest!" exclaimed Jennifer. "What kind of contest?"

"Illusions. You'll each conjure one, and I'll pick a winner based on originality, difficulty, and execution." Perry was frowning. "And," he

9

added, "your age will be taken into account."

Perry brightened. "Sounds good to me," he said.

"Listen to him," sniffed Jennifer. "As if being the youngest will help."

"My chances are better than some people's."

"Ha! Why, I'll—"

"That's enough squabbling," said the Professor. "Save your energy for the contest. Now, who'll go first?"

"I will," volunteered Jamie.

He closed his eyes.

Without warning, a tremendous bear lumbered up over the hill. His clothes were even more striking than his size; not every bear wears a tuxedo and top hat.

The stylish bear came forward, bowing deeply to his assembled audience. Removing his hat, he waved a paw over it and pulled out a rabbit. Apparently dissatisfied, he put the rabbit down and shook the hat fiercely. Nothing more came out. The bear dropped the hat to the ground. He pried it open and stuck in his snout. The further he looked, the more of him the hat swallowed up. Soon only his feet were left, kicking blindly at the air. Then they, too, were gone. The hat spun wildly on the grass, a black blur that faded slowly until it disappeared.

The rabbit hopped away.

"Well done, Jamie," said Edward. "That will be hard to beat."

Alison stood up determinedly. "I'll go next," she said.

A flock of swans glided overhead, forming a giant circle against the sky. Each one carried a bouquet of flowers in his bill. One after another, they dipped their long necks and dropped the bouquets. The flowers drifted down on the wind, dissolving in a rainbow of colors.

The swans veered westward, their feathers glowing softly in the reflection of the setting sun. As the glow brightened, they vanished like a display of fireworks.

"Beautiful," said Jennifer.

Alison, though, looked more puzzled than pleased. "The swans weren't supposed to explode," she murmured.

"Don't complain," whispered Jamie. "Father was impressed."

"But still . . ."

"Be quiet and watch Edward."

Edward conjured up five circus clowns. They popped in and out of hoops, somersaulted between three invisible trapezes, and leaped on each other's shoulders to form a giant pyramid.

"Looks like a rocket," said Jamie.

As if on cue, the clowns blasted off into the sky. Higher and higher they went, finally vanishing into the clouds.

Those same clouds served Jennifer next. At her bidding, the fluffy shapes rearranged themselves into an angry bull pawing the ground before a waiting matador. The matador looked splendid whirling his cape expertly in the path of his horned opponent. Again and again the bull charged, only to be deftly turned aside by his agile foe. The exhibition continued until a gust of wind came by and dissolved the participants.

"The competition is stiff, indeed," said the Professor evenly. "It's your turn, Perry. Are you ready?"

"Yes, Father." Perry turned to a nearby apple tree and slowly raised his arms.

In the spring, apple trees bloom with white blossoms, and this one was no different from the rest, at least not until that moment. But then Perry transformed it. Apples appeared on the branches, ripening in seconds, then fell to the ground in tempting piles.

The Professor laughed. "Wishful thinking, Perry," he said, "but a good idea nonetheless." He paused. "All things considered, I proclaim you the winner."

Perry beamed at Jennifer.

She glared at him in return. "Now that you've won," she muttered, "you can stop it already."

"But I have stopped," Perry insisted.

"Well, the tree hasn't gotten the message."

A small lake of apples was growing as new ones continued to rain down from the branches.

"I'm not doing it," said Perry. "Honest."

Professor Wynd frowned and spread his fingers toward the tree. The air shimmered. Then the apples vanished, and the white blossoms of May returned.

"What happened, Father?" asked Edward.

"The illusion extended itself. Somehow, it took on an independent course."

"So did mine," said Alison. "The swans were only supposed to fly away, not explode."

"You're certain, Alison?" the Professor asked.

"Oh, yes. Making swans explode would be a terrible idea."

13

Her father nodded. "It's an odd coincidence," he said. "Of course, they may have been magical quirks. Such things do happen. Anyway," he added, noting the lengthening shadows in the grass, "it's getting late. Time we started back."

The trip home was a quiet one; everyone was busy wondering about the runaway illusions. A quirk was just a quirk, but what if it were something else?

TWO

ALL DAY Sunday Professor Wynd sat in his study. Occasionally he stood up to look out the window, and once he watered the plants, but mostly he just sat, idly staring at his cathedral notes. As a specialist in medieval studies at Berkshire College, he was currently writing an essay on gargoyles, but his thoughts kept wandering to the events of the day before. The Professor was not satisfied with explaining away the spells' behavior as mere magical quirks. The whole thing left him uneasy.

Absently, he fiddled with the small porcelain gargoyles sitting on a shelf above his desk. There were twelve of them, a gift from a colleague who was amused by the Professor's choice of research. The intricately cast models were scaled reproductions of those gargoyles still guarding cathedrals, palaces, and the like all over Europe. They had a gruesome sort of appeal, a kind of rough-hewn charm. Probably good fighters, thought the Professor, noting their grim expressions, though perhaps not very bright. Removing them from the shelf, he arranged the creatures in two columns on his desk. It was a military formation, maybe without the regimental spit and polish of tin soldiers, but military nonetheless.

The Professor addressed his troops. "Gentlemen," he began, hoping the term would not offend them, "I am unable to concentrate on my work, work that concerns you all, simply because of some puzzling illusions I saw yesterday." He twirled his index finger at them. "What should I do about it?"

The gargoyles said nothing. Gargoyles rarely do, of course, and only when sufficiently provoked. Such was not the case.

"Come now," said the Professor, "there's no reason you can't speak up. Maybe you need a little encouragement." He lightly touched the two foremost gargoyles and murmured a spell.

The change was quickly apparent. The milky smoothness of the porcelain surface swirled and shifted into a leathery gray skin. The glazed eyes softened and blinked repeatedly.

After a moment, one of the gargoyles suddenly twitched. He staggered forward unsteadily, fluttering his wings for balance and making scratchy cries in his throat. Wandering across the desk, he soon reached a pencil, a curiosity he immediately tried to eat. The other gargoyle was slower, but after a few timid steps, he marched briskly toward his companion, who was now gnawing an eraser.

The Professor motioned to the remaining figures, who sputtered to a start like rusty wind-up toys. They crawled over the blotter, scattering pens and papers in their path.

The edge of the desk posed the greatest mystery. One inquiring fellow, still wobbly on his feet, accidentally fell off while investigating it. His wings, though, opened at once, lifting the surprised gargoyle to the ceiling.

The Professor laughed. "Here now," he said, "this isn't an aviary. You'll have to come down."

The gargoyle refused; he was too busy exploring his new terrain. It must have appealed to him, because he began chirping to the others. Singly and in pairs they sought the air as well. Several gargoyles nosed among the shelves, knocking over a small vase and sending a row of books tumbling to the floor. Two of them, like daredevil fliers, repeatedly plummeted to the carpet, always pulling up safely at the last moment.

Things were getting out of hand. Once more the Professor said, "Come down!"

The gargoyles ignored him.

The Professor tried to grab one, but only had his hand nipped for his efforts. And the annoyed gargoyle was not finished with him. Rising to the ceiling, he suddenly dove at the Professor, who snatched up a book to shield himself. More gargoyles joined the fray, buzzing like a swarm of angry bees. Hoping to stop the gargoyles harmlessly, Professor Wynd tried some gentle spells, but with no success. Finally, he had to resort to a very firm enchantment.

The gargoyles hovered in place, frozen in time. Their features hardened, the textured gray hue giving way to the shinier porcelain finish. But, as the Professor had feared might be the case, the transformation was too abrupt—the gargoyles exploded in powdery bursts, showering the study with ceramic dust. Shaking his head, the Professor brushed off his shoulders.

The door banged open as Jamie and Jennifer rushed into the room. They glanced around quizzically. "What happened, Father?" Jamie asked. "We heard you shout."

"A small accident, nothing more."

Nothing more looked like quite a bit to Jennifer. "What about all this dust?" she asked. "The room's filled with the stuff. And . . ." She paused, staring at the desk. "Father, the gargoyles are gone! Did—"

"Jennifer," he said sharply, "save your questions for another time. I appreciate your concern, but I've work to do. Close your mouth, Jamie. No questions from you, either. Now run along, my two fine mother hens."

He shut the door behind them and turned back to survey the room. "No need to worry anyone else," he thought. "Not yet, anyway."

THREE

LATE MONDAY afternoon, Perry was standing on the stage of the Westbridge Elementary School auditorium. It was not where he wanted to be. He would much rather have been investigating the wayward spells. The idea of something messing around with one of his enchantments still bothered him. And although he had searched unsuccessfully for clues on Sunday, he hoped to find an explanation—if only the stupid play rehearsal would end.

All about him were the trappings of an ancient royal chamber: a high-backed throne, silver candelabra, and a red carpet. As King Arthur, Perry was fidgeting with his scepter at the edge of the curtain.

"Perry!"

He jerked to attention.

"I must remind you, Perry," said his teacher,

Mrs. Hartwick, "to stand closer to your queen. Nancy doesn't have the plague, you know. And she can hardly hear your lines when you're way over there. Besides, you love her deeply, remember? You want to be at her side, not the curtain's. That's it, that's much better."

Grumbling to himself, the King edged closer to Queen Guinevere, who was waiting impatiently by the throne.

"All right, Nancy," said Mrs. Hartwick, "start from where we left off. And don't forget, this is one of the world's classic romances."

"Oh, Arthur," sighed the Queen rapturously, "must you depart so soon?"

"I fear so, my dear," he answered, trying to muster the proper concern. "There is evil abroad in the land. My subjects suffer greatly, and I have pledged to do battle on their behalf. It is my sworn duty."

Queen Guinevere looked away sadly. "Then I can only wish you godspeed and pray for your quick return."

"Fear not for my safety," said the King, touching her gingerly on the shoulder.

"Perry," growled Mrs. Hartwick, "the Queen is your beloved wife, not some dead animal you slew on a hunt. Try to keep that in mind. Show her the affection I know you're capable of."

The King made a face and tried again. "Fear not for my safety, dearest Guinevere. I have my magic sword, Excalibur, and my trusty knights to protect me from any harm."

Silence.

"George!" shouted Mrs. Hartwick. "That's your cue."

A page stumbled out from behind the curtain and approached the royal couple, bowing deeply. "I beg pardon for this profusion, Majesties," he gasped.

"No, George," said Mrs. Hartwick. "I've told you before. Not profusion. Intrusion. Begin again."

George cleared his throat. "I beg pardon for this intrusion, Majesties," he said.

"Rise and state your message," said the King.

"Sire, the dragons are attacking the Westlands, slaughtering the sheep and burning the villages."

The King frowned. "This is grave news indeed," he declared. "I will leave forthwith."

"Oh, Arthur," said the Queen, "do be careful."

The subject of her ardor stepped to the front of the stage. "I must defend England from her foes," he said stoutly, pulling Excalibur from his scabbard. The sword, cut from plywood and covered with aluminum foil, glinted in a shaft of sunlight. The King brandished it menacingly. "Woe be onto the enemies of our realm. With my trusty sword, Excalibur, I shall rout the dragons from our midst!" he shouted. It was Perry's favorite line.

As Perry said these words, a tongue of flame licked the tip of his sword. When he mentioned "dragons," the whole blade flickered with a white fire. A moment later, the fire was gone. Strangely, it left no trace of its presence behind; Excalibur was not burned or charred in any way.

The Queen screamed.

Mrs. Hartwick jumped up from her seat. "Calm down, Nancy," she said nervously. "There's nothing to be frightened about. Everything's all right."

"B-but I saw flames," sniffed Nancy.

"Now, Nancy, you only thought you saw flames. How could the sword have been on fire? That's impossible. Perry's not upset, and he was holding the sword. It was just a trick of the light. A trick of the light," she repeated, as though to convince herself.

Perry wasn't upset about the sword, but only

because he was too angry. One of his brothers or sisters, he thought, had to be responsible for that trick, and whoever it was would regret it.

Mrs. Hartwick was fanning herself with the text of the play. "Well, well," she fluttered, "perhaps we've practiced enough for today. Study your lines tonight, and we'll continue with Act III tomorrow afternoon."

PERRY RUSHED HOME, to find the others playing croquet in the backyard.

"Which one of you was it?" he demanded.

"Which one of us was what?" asked Jamie.

Perry kicked a stake. "You know what I'm talking about!" he shouted.

"Be quiet, Perry," said Jennifer. "You're spoiling my concentration. I have to be careful if I'm going to poison Alison without passing through a wicket."

"I won't be quiet! I want to know who did it, and I want to know now!"

Edward put down his mallet. "Honestly, Perry, I don't know what you're talking about. We've been playing croquet for the last hour. Jennifer's won every game. We think she cheats, but we haven't figured out how."

"Cheats? Who cheats?" cried Jennifer.

"Simmer down, Jenny," said Alison. "He's

only teasing, I think."

"But it had to be one of you," Perry insisted.

"It wasn't," said Alison.

"We don't even know what happened," said Jamie.

Perry told them. The story left the others as puzzled as he was.

"I don't have any explanations," said Edward, "but none of us were there."

Jennifer glanced around warily. "You don't suppose it's all part of a larger pattern?" she asked.

"Don't be melodramatic," said Alison.

"I'm not sure she's wrong," said Jamie. "Yesterday, Jenny and I heard a commotion in the study. When we looked in, we found Father standing by his desk, all upset. The air was filled with dust, and his little gargoyles were missing. I know something strange happened in there, something Father wouldn't tell us about. And if it's connected to this . . ."

"The one thing we know is that magic is involved," said Jennifer. "I think we should look into the matter. Let's convene the Council."

"I agree," said Perry, and only rarely did he agree with Jennifer.

Alison nodded slowly. "I guess you're right," she said. "We'll meet after dinner tonight."

FOUR

THE COUNCIL CHAMBER in the attic was shared with a family of spiders, but they kept mostly to the rafters. It was a comfortable place, filled with family relics and old furniture now too ragged for downstairs. Great-Uncle William's harpoon rested in one corner, not far from Grandmother Wynd's first sewing machine; and a raccoon coat, no longer the fashion, covered the shoulders of a suit of armor, which looked gallant nonetheless.

When they were all seated, Jennifer convened the Council. It was her turn to chair the proceedings and she clearly relished the job. No one else was so fascinated by the details of parliamentary procedure.

"Here's the problem—" began Perry.

"Silence!" commanded Jennifer. "You're out of order. You haven't been recognized by the Chair."

"Don't be stupid, Jenny," Perry fumed. "Chairs can't recognize people. Even you should know better than that."

The Chair rolled her eyes in exasperation.

"May I have leave to speak?" asked Alison, humoring her sister's love of propriety.

The Chair said that she might.

"Well," said Alison, "we all know something peculiar has been going on lately; first there were the spells, then whatever happened in Father's study, and now Perry's flaming sword. If a common thread connects the three, we must discover it."

The Council murmured its agreement.

"The motion is accepted for consideration," said Jennifer solemnly. "The Chair now opens the floor to general debate. Yes, Edward?"

"Father once told me that powerful beings can disturb nearby spells, if their own magic is working. Sort of like a stone thrown in a pool causing ripples."

Jamie snickered. "Other beings?" he said. "Don't be ridiculous. Wouldn't we know about them?"

"We practice magic in secret," Edward observed. "Somebody else could do that as well."

This was an unpleasant thought. The Wynds studied magic quietly, without any fuss. But somebody else might do it very differently.

"If that's true, how can we find who's responsible?" asked Perry. "Where should we look?"

"And even if we do find him or her or them," said Jamie, "then what?"

No one had a ready answer.

"Oh, dear," gulped Jennifer in a very undignified way. "What if it isn't a *somebody?* What if it's a *something?*"

The thought made their blood run cold.

"Don't let your imagination get out of hand," said Alison primly. "After all, this isn't the Middle Ages or some dark, deserted isle. It's the twentieth century. Any monsters on the prowl could hardly be overlooked these days. They'd be spotted by radar or something."

"We haven't been spotted by radar," said Edward soberly. "The possibility of a monster may be fantastic, but then the whole thing is fantastic."

Such talk was unsettling. The Council members fidgeted uncomfortably.

"Order! Order!" cried Jennifer, banging an

old hammer on the cracker barrel that served as a podium. "Let's not sit here all mopey," she said. "I know what we can do. We will summon the magical being, if there is one, to appear before us. Like a seance."

"Of all the daffy ideas," said Perry. "Huddled around like fortunetellers, crying, 'Oh, dearie, sppeeaak to us from the sppiirrriiit world.' "

"Wait a minute, Perry," said Edward. "I've read of such things being done successfully. It might work for us, if there is someone or something around causing trouble. Besides, have you got a better idea?"

Perry had to admit he didn't.

"Since the objections have been removed," said Jennifer, "let's get started. Edward, do you know what we'll need? Good. You'll be in charge. The Council will be in recess for one hour."

The hammer rapped sharply on the barrel.

That hour was spent frantically searching the house for the necessary props. Normally, Professor Wynd would have questioned such frenzied activity, but he was at work in his study, oblivious to the tramping of feet up and down the stairs.

Edward and Jennifer were just making the final arrangements when the clock struck nine. The attic was a changed place. Dark blankets hung from the walls and ceiling, forming a pentagon-shaped enclosure. The floor was covered with magical symbols and signs, their colors shifting under the light of the oil lantern hanging from the rafters. The lantern rocked gently, casting shadows that flickered almost with a life of their own.

Jamie watched them warily. "You don't think anything would come here uninvited, do you?" he asked.

"Well," said Alison, "demons and ghosts are probably too busy with their own affairs to bother with us. Of course, I suppose a few might come to watch."

"And if they do?"

"We'll tell them to watch quietly. I'm sure demons can be reasonable."

"Hooow doo yoouu knoow?" asked Perry.

"Cut it out, Perry," said Jamie. "This isn't the time to fool around."

"Why don't we begin?" said Alison quickly.

"All right," said Edward, checking everything one last time. He glanced at the barrel, the lantern, the checkered tablecloth, and finally the inverted fishbowl. The latter he eyed doubtfully. "Jamie, was this the closest thing to a crystal sphere you could find?"

"Crystal spheres don't grow on trees, you know," Jamie replied sharply. "It was either the fishbowl or one of those snow-filled paperweights."

Edward sighed. "Let's hope magical beings aren't sticklers for detail."

The children sat in a small circle around the barrel. "Now," said Edward, "we must all clasp hands and concentrate on the, ah, crystal sphere. I will then start the ceremony with Jennifer's assistance."

Jennifer placed a silver cup next to the crystal sphere.

"Hey!" exclaimed Perry. "That's mine! Grandfather gave it to—"

"Be quiet!" ordered Jennifer. "You'll ruin everything. We aren't going to hurt your precious cup. It was just the only silver one we could find."

"To continue," said Edward. "Stare into the crystal sphere. Let it fill your mind. And remember, if anyone breaks the chain of hands, the spell will break, too."

He nodded to Jennifer, who poured a specially prepared powder into the silver cup. A dark liquid was added, and the resulting mixture bubbled and fizzed furiously. Wisps of smoke, smelling vaguely of sulfur and charcoal, filtered through the room.

"I'll never get the smell of rotten eggs out of that cup," Perry muttered to himself.

Edward's eyes became glassy and distant. The lantern light brightened as he said:

We summon forth the magic being,
Whom we have felt, but have not seen.
So please appear now in this place,
Then we can meet you, face to face.

The *please* had been Jamie's idea. He thought it might help to be polite.

Everyone sat very quietly, hardly daring even to breathe. For a terribly long minute or two, nothing happened. Perry stirred uncomfortably, and Jamie's nose itched, but he tried to ignore it.

Suddenly, Edward's face grew pale, and a deep chill settled on the room. The blankets billowed noisily.

"Look!" cried Jennifer.

The center of the fishbowl glowed with a bright light. The children all blinked, thinking maybe they were imagining it; but the light was real. It was not the steady kind a bulb radiates, more like the fiercely changing flames in the middle of a roaring fire.

"I feel as if I'm being watched," murmured Alison.

The light now filled the fishbowl; the fiery glow brushed the edges of the glass. The shimmering air danced on the children's faces. They sat unable to move, unable to speak.

Then the awful silence was pierced by Jennifer. An eye was glaring at her from the midst of the sphere. She screamed, jumping up from her seat. The eye blinked once, and the light vanished.

FIVE

NONE of the children spent a particularly restful night, and the morning did not improve their mood. The abrupt end of the seance had unsettled them, but not because they wished it had gone on. As Edward said, he wasn't sorry Jennifer had broken the chain. In those last moments he had sensed a very powerful and unfriendly presence. And that was something to worry about.

THAT AFTERNOON, after muddling through another rehearsal, Perry walked to the library in Westbridge. At Mrs. Hartwick's urging, he was going to do some background reading on Camelot, in the hope it would make him feel more at ease with Queen Guinevere. However, since it wasn't the Queen, but Nancy Abbott, who prompted his uneasiness, Perry didn't think the reading would help. But he did as he was told.

Westbridge looked like a picture postcard of a New England village. Stores and shops bordered three sides of a large green, and the fourth faced a simple eighteenth century church. Beyond the church was the library, a stone mansion built by the town some years before.

After an hour lost in a world filled with chivalry and jousts, gallant deeds and songs, Perry decided he was as comfortable with Queen Guinevere as he would ever be. He left the library and wandered over to the post office, where a small group of people had gathered around Charlie Fisher. Charlie was a farmer, but Perry knew him as the chief of Westbridge's volunteer fire department. Sometimes he let Perry ride on the truck during practice drills.

"I tell you it happened!" exclaimed Charlie as Perry came up.

"Sure you did," agreed Ned Witherspoon, proprietor of Witherspoon's Hardware Store. "And you told it well." He winked broadly at the others. "But can you tell it the same way twice?"

"Of course, I can," said Charlie defiantly. "I

woke up around three o'clock this morning
. . ."

"Upset stomach?" asked Bill Smathers, one of
the cooks at the Westbridge Inn. Charlie was
known as a poor hand in the kitchen.

"It so happens I ate at the Inn last night,"
Charlie retorted. "But it wasn't my stomach.
My herd was restless, the chickens were
cackling, and my dog, Sam, was howling up a
storm. I thought maybe a fox was on the prowl,
so I took a look."

"And what did you find?" asked Bill

Charlie took a deep breath. "Well," he said,
"it was dark, but there's no mistaking what I
saw. Some kind of beast was lifting my prize
heifer, Martha, off the ground. Martha was bel-
lowing like crazy. I went back for my rifle, but
the beast was gone when I returned."

"Lifted Martha off the ground . . ." Bill repeated. "You mean the beast was flying?"

"That's right."

Bill snorted. "You must have dreamed it."

"No, I didn't," Charlie insisted. "I checked
the herd this morning. Martha's gone."

"Did you look for her?" Bill asked. "Maybe
she just wandered off."

"I didn't have to," Charlie replied. "There
was dried blood all over the spot where the

beast took her. Lots of it."

Ned Witherspoon shook his head. "You tell a good story, Charlie, I'll grant you that."

"I know what I saw," said Charlie angrily. "If the rest of you don't believe me, that's your lookout."

"Aw, Charlie," said Bill, "you oughta be ashamed. Look, your fool story scared the kid."

Admittedly, Perry had darted across the green, but not because Charlie Fisher's story had frightened him. Perry thrived on wild tales. His problem was something else, or rather, someone else—namely, Nancy Abbott. She had spotted him from the other side of the street. If Perry hadn't been listening to the story so intently, he would have seen her earlier and hidden somewhere. Now it was too late for that.

But there was still time to run. Nancy called out to him, but Perry ignored her. Putting up with those rehearsals was bad enough, he wasn't about to sacrifice the rest of his day, too. As he passed the church, Perry glanced back; Nancy had taken up the chase. She was pretty fast, but Perry was inspired. He spurted ahead, dashing toward the woods between two nearby hills.

When he next looked around, there was no

sign of her. Perry listened anxiously for foot-steps. He knew how tricky girls could be. But the only sound he heard was his heart pounding like a bass drum.

Then a twig snapped. "Could be a rabbit," he thought nervously, "or . . ." Not one to take chances, Perry ducked inside the mouth of a cave.

He waited. After a few minutes of silence, Perry sighed thankfully. He was about to leave when he realized the cave was new to him, though he had explored the area many times before. "How could I have missed this?" he wondered, as he set off to correct his oversight.

The cave was actually a long tunnel, sloping downward under the hill. Moving slowly in the gray twilight, Perry soon reached a fork. To the right, it was completely dark; to the left, there was a dim light from up ahead. Cautiously, he entered the left-hand passage. The light brightened with every step.

"Oh, my!" he gasped, stopping abruptly at the rim of a large underground cavern. Fiery torches hung from the walls, but even more surprising was what covered the cavern floor: treasure chests piled with gold and silver coins, kingly crowns, gems, and jewel-encrusted swords, to name just some of it.

Perry took a deep breath and inspected his find. He tried on a few crowns for size, but they all perched ignobly on the bridge of his nose. While struggling to lift a great broadsword, he tottered onto a basket of silk brocade, entangling himself in the shiny cloth.

Sitting down rather abruptly, he began tossing rubies and amethysts into a gold flagon until it suddenly occurred to him that torches don't light themselves. Whoever this treasure belonged to might be right around the corner. Probably pirates, he thought. It wouldn't do to be captured by pirates. Hastily, Perry dropped the flagon, got up, ran to the tunnel entrance, and hurried home.

JENNIFER LAUGHED. "Come on, Perry, or should I say, Ali Baba? The sword was one thing, but we're not going to swallow this. I mean, treasure in a mysterious underground cavern? That doesn't even happen in books anymore."

"I don't expect you to swallow anything!" Perry shouted. "I'm telling the truth. It must be pirate treasure. The pirates are somewhere nearby, I guess."

"We want to be reasonable," said Jamie.

"You couldn't bring back a whole pirate, I suppose, but you might have managed a doubloon or two. Or maybe a couple of emeralds."

"I'm not particular," snickered Jennifer. "A diamond, a small one, would have satisfied me."

"Very funny," Perry said wearily. "And here I rushed home to tell you about it, so we could all go back to the cave tomorrow." He glared at Jennifer. "Then you can pick out your own diamond."

"Ha!" she trumpeted.

Perry sighed. "Don't you believe me, Alison?" he asked.

Alison suppressed a grin. "I'd like to," she said, "but it's difficult. After all, you're talking about pirates in the Berkshires. Hardly the spot you'd expect to find them. And, if you don't mind my asking, where are they keeping their ship?"

Perry hadn't considered the ship. "I don't know. Maybe they don't have a ship."

"Oh sure," said Jamie. "Pirates without a ship. That makes heaps of sense."

Perry ignored him. "What about you, Edward?" he asked.

"Well, Perry, you have been known to

stretch the truth occasionally, but I'll keep an open mind until you get some proof."

"Ooooh!" exploded Perry. "You're all as bad as Ned Witherspoon!"

"What's that supposed to mean?" sneered Jennifer.

"Never mind. Just be here tomorrow at four o'clock. I'll bring you your precious proof."

SIX

AFTER REHEARSAL the next day, Perry headed directly for the cave. He found it easily and made his way quickly to the cavern. The treasure looked even larger than before. Perry figured he could ransom kings, maybe whole countries, with all the stuff in there. But what he needed now was just a little proof of its existence, something to crush the doubts of his brothers and sisters. For that purpose, he had brought along his sword, Excalibur, in his bookbag. A newly jeweled hilt would impress the others, even Jennifer.

A small chest of sapphires and diamonds caught Perry's eye, and he moved toward it. But in doing so, he tripped over a spiked crown, tumbling noisily into a mound of silver coins. He slowly got to his feet, rubbing his shoulder in pain. Silver coins are not the most comfortable things to fall on.

"What have we here?" asked a deep voice behind him.

Perry spun around and gaped at what he saw. A terrifying beast towered above him. He was at least fifteen feet tall, and every one of those feet was covered with shiny scales. A line of thick spikes ran along his back and down his long tail. On either side of the spikes was a leathery wing. Perry didn't notice the wings at first; he was concentrating on the toothy snout.

"Who are you?" asked the dragon, for so the beast had always been called.

"A boy," mumbled Perry. "A harmless little boy, hardly worth mentioning."

"Humph!" snorted the dragon. "Harmless, eh? And since when are thieves harmless?"

"I'm not a thief!" Perry insisted.

"No? Then what are you doing here?"

Perry paused. The beast might not understand the difference between what he was doing and thievery. Maybe if the beast had a family . . . but Perry was afraid to ask. Quite possibly, he wouldn't be interested in such details. Still, the question had to be answered.

"I only came back to explore," he said. This was not the exact truth, but that was the last thing on Perry's mind.

The smoke billowed from the dragon's snout. "Back?" he thundered. "Are you saying you've been here before? Well, answer me. Are you?"

Perry nodded nervously. "Yesterday," he said. Not sure the beast wanted to hear all about his narrow escape from Nancy Abbott, he explained as briefly as he could.

The dragon displayed a polite interest. "A stirring tale," he said dryly when Perry had finished. "But tell me, is this Nancy a fair damsel?"

Perry had certainly never thought of her that way. "Nobody has ever called her one," he said, and then added, "but she's only nine."

"A bit young," the dragon admitted. "Too bad. I'm rather partial to fair damsels. It's only natural for a dragon."

Perry gulped. "Did you say *dragon?*" he asked.

"Of course, I said *dragon,*" snapped the dragon. "As if I could be confused with anything else." He rippled his scales admiringly. "And I'm a particularly fine one at that. It's no wonder they call me Shimmerscale."

Had Perry known more about dragons, at that point he would have added a flattering appraisal of his own. His thoughts, though, were about dinner; not his—Shimmerscale's. Perry didn't know what kind of meal he would make, and he didn't want to find out. Inching his way toward a small gap between the dragon and the tunnel, he watched for his chance to bolt.

But dragons, even vain ones, are not that careless. "Don't hurry off," said Shimmerscale pointedly. His spiked tail thumped down before Perry, blocking the gap completely. "We must have a little chat first."

Perry shrank back against the cavern wall.

Shimmerscale looked fiercely into his eyes. "You need not fear if you answer me truthfully. Now tell me, how many men in your village? How many knights guard the castle?"

Perry blinked under the dragon's continued stare. "I won't tell you anything," he declared stoutly.

Shimmerscale sighed. "If I took the time, you would tell me whatever I wished to know, and many things I haven't the slightest interest in. But dragons are not noted for their patience, and I am no exception. So, I will settle for a cruder, more direct, approach." His tail flicked toward Perry, scratching an arc in the stone around him.

A moment later the arc burst into flame.

"Let me explain the situation," Shimmer-

45

scale said slowly, pausing over each word to watch Perry squirm. "The endpoints of the arc are fixed, but every time you refuse to answer a question, the arc will straighten out a little, eventually becoming flush with the wall. But long before then, you will get in the way; with what result you can no doubt imagine."

Shimmerscale was right about that. Already the flames were close enough for Perry to toast marshmallows. Any closer and he could do it without the stick.

"If you now choose to be reasonable," the dragon added confidently, "I will put the fire out."

Put the fire out. The words pierced Perry's fright. He suddenly remembered he could do that himself, and conjured the proper spell at once.

The fiery arc snuffed itself out.

Shimmerscale snorted in rage. "Magic!" he exclaimed. "From a mere boy? Apparently there are more important questions to ask you."

Perry stared at him defiantly. "It won't do any good," he said, feeling very pleased with himself.

"We shall see," growled the dragon. "You are

young to be a sorcerer's apprentice, and certainly your powers can be no match for mine."

Something touched Perry's thoughts, searching for the information that lay there. He recoiled instinctively, but could not escape the thrust of the mind probe. It was a very old and difficult kind of magic to work, and painful for the victim, as Perry was finding out.

The magical defenses against such probes were beyond Perry's skill, but he was not limited to magic alone. He knew that mind probes could sometimes be blocked by the strength of a single overpowering thought. So Perry concentrated on his father, and the comforting image shielded him from Shimmerscale's spell.

The frustrated dragon was infuriated by Perry's stubborn resistance. Shimmerscale had not faced a real confrontation in a long time, but still . . .

The probe lashed out again.

"Ooooh," Perry groaned, and slumped to the ground unconscious.

SEVEN

A S THE CLOCK struck five, Alison looked up from the book she was reading. "Perry should have been here by now," she said. "I wonder what's keeping him."

"He's an hour late," said Jennifer, stalking the floor impatiently. "Probably hiding somewhere. Made the whole story up, and now he's afraid to face us. Wait till I get my hands on him."

"I'm not so sure," said Edward. "I've been thinking about his story. It was different from his others. I mean, he usually tries to make them believable. He didn't come close this time."

"And he was really angry," Jamie added. "It was no act."

Alison frowned. "I hope he's all right. Maybe we should go look for him."

"Hmmph!" muttered Jennifer. "What a bunch of softies. If you ask me, looking for him is a waste of time. But I suppose it won't do us any harm."

"Let's start in town," suggested Edward. "Somebody there may have seen him."

Twenty minutes later, they crossed the village green. One of the few people strolling under the darkening sky was Bill Smathers, who had just finished his shift at the Inn. He watched the children approach.

"Good evening, Mr. Smathers," said Edward.

"Evening. It's young Edward Wynd, isn't it? Well, I don't often see such a sampling of your family. How's the Professor and the Missus?"

"Fine, thank you," Edward replied. "Mr. Smathers, have you by any chance seen our little brother, Perry, today?"

"Can't say that I have. But I believe he was in town yesterday." Bill rubbed his chin thoughtfully. "I remember now. 'Round four o'clock it was, or maybe a bit before. That Charlie Fisher was spinning a yarn to me, and Ned and—"

"Excuse me," said Alison. "Was that Ned Witherspoon?"

"That's right."

"Did Mr. Witherspoon believe the story?" asked Jennifer, fidgeting guiltily.

Bill chuckled. "I should think not," he said. "It was a real whopper about one of Charlie's cows mysteriously disappearing in the night. Your brother was listening quietly, and then he ran away. I figured the story had scared him, but there was this little girl hot on his heels. I don't know which he was running from."

"Long blond pigtails?" asked Jennifer.

"I think so. Cute little thing."

"That's Nancy Abbott," said Jamie.

"Mr. Smathers, did you happen to see which way Perry went?" Alison asked.

"As a matter of fact, I did. He ran up Springfield Road toward Charlie's farm." Bill smiled. "He's quick, your brother."

While Bill spoke, Jennifer nudged Edward, motioning for him to look skyward. As he looked, a dark form, half-hidden in the drizzling twilight, darted through the blackened clouds.

"Well, ah, thank you, Mr. Smathers," Edward said quickly. "We'll just keep looking."

He and Jennifer led the others away.

"Jenny, stop poking me so mysteriously," said Alison. "Whatever is the matter?"

"She spotted something in the sky," said Edward. "Some kind of beast. It's hidden in the clouds now, but it might come down at any moment."

"Did you get a good look?" asked Jamie. "Maybe it was a large bird."

Jennifer shuddered. "That was no bird," she said.

"There it is again!" cried Edward.

Certainly, no bird ever looked like that. But then, dragons have never claimed to resemble birds; they don't look like anything but what they are.

Jamie glanced around. "No one else seems to have noticed him yet," he observed. "Luckily there aren't many people outside."

"Anyone who did see him," said Edward, "probably wouldn't believe it. I'm having trouble myself. Who would have thought a dragon would be flying over Westbridge."

"Dragon?" exclaimed the others. Impossible, they thought; but the truth, of course, was that the impossible really was gliding over their heads. His name was Quickblast, a young, impulsive dragon who was getting some exercise before snaring another cow.

Jamie's eyes glowed with excitement. "If the dragon attacks," he said, "we'll defend the town till victory is ours!"

"We'll be heroes," said Jennifer.

Neither Jamie nor Jennifer had had any experience fighting dragons, which explains their cheery outlook. Veteran dragon fighters (what few there are) are not a cheery lot.

"Heroics are all very fine," said Edward, "but what if we're seen using magic?"

"If we combine our strength in a single spell," said Alison, "we can freeze the townspeople for a few minutes. They won't remember it afterwards, and we can deal with the dragon in the meantime."

"Makes sense," agreed Edward. "Let's do it quickly. We don't know what the dragon has in mind."

The spell spread slowly outward, drifting through the town like gentle wisps of smoke. The most unfortunate victim was little Julie Tyler, who froze while eating a popsicle (unfortunate because unlike herself, the popsicle did not freeze, but melted all over her dress).

A roll of thunder rumbled in the distance. Almost in answer, the bell in the church belfry struck five-thirty, and the Westminster chimes signaled the half-hour. Thunder was a familiar sound to Quickblast; it didn't disturb him. The church bells were a different matter. Quickblast knew nothing of Westminster chimes, and he found the strange ringing somewhat frightening. Interpreting the sound as a call to battle, the dragon attacked. Roaring fire like some living comet, Quickblast plunged from the cloud cover, hurtling toward the defenseless belfry. With his great claws extended, the red and orange flames surging from his snout, he clove the church tower neatly in two. The groaning crunch of splintered wood was a more pleasing music to his ears.

"How will we explain that?" asked Jennifer as another roll of thunder rumbled by.

"We won't have to," said Jamie. "Everyone will think lightning struck the church during the storm."

Alison nodded. "True," she said, "but if the dragon wrecks the whole town, it will be difficult to blame the lightning alone."

"Then let's make sure he doesn't," said Edward. "First, of course, we have to bring him down." He cupped his hands together, and a gray mist issued from the spot. It snaked toward the unsuspecting Quickblast, who was hovering near the church, proudly surveying the destruction. The mist drew closer around him, hardening into silver rings, stronger than steel, pinning his wings to his side. Without the use of his wings, Quickblast plummeted to the ground.

The children cheered, thinking the dragon was their prisoner. But if dragons were that easy to defeat, they could hardly lay claim to their fearsome reputations.

Despite his undignified fall, Quickblast was unharmed. He couldn't break the rings with sheer force, but dragons have other means at their disposal. Engulfing his bonds in a sheet of flame, Quickblast melted them instantly. He was not burned in the process because dragons are immune to their own fire.

Spreading his wings with renewed strength, Quickblast rose from the ground, climbing to a great height over the village. His sharp ears had noted the cheers accompanying his fall. Whoever had challenged him would soon regret it.

Edward was regretting it already. He had watched in astonishment as the dragon freed himself, knowing that the spell joining those rings would have withstood the heat of an iron foundry. What Edward didn't know was that dragon-fire has properties foundry fires don't.

"If it's fire he wants," said Jennifer, "it's fire

he'll get." A large fireball mushroomed in her hand, and she threw it determinedly at the darkened form overhead. The fireball blazed upward, the image of a shooting star with a poor sense of direction. It burst suddenly upon Quickblast's snout, exploding like a fireworks display and showering him with sparks. The startled dragon howled in pain as the magical flames danced before his eyes.

"That's showing him," said Jamie approvingly, thumping his sister on the back.

"It's showing him where we are, anyway," said Edward, taking the more practical view.

It certainly was, and the enraged dragon cast aside any careful plan of attack, choosing to wreak immediate vengeance on his troublesome foes. With the wind whistling at his back and flames streaming behind him, Quickblast dove toward the children below.

"The hydrant, Jamie! The hydrant!" cried Alison.

Jamie motioned to the fire hydrant at the corner of the green, whirling his finger counterclockwise. Its cap unscrewed. The water gushed out, shooting upward, a powerful fountain aimed at the descending dragon. This was Alison's doing, and she did it well.

The fountain smacked into Quickblast with a loud hiss, momentarily obscuring him in steamy clouds. When the air cleared, the dragon could be seen hovering dismally above the treetops. The water dripped unbecomingly from his snout. More importantly, his fire had been quenched. Quickblast was mortified that such a thing should happen, and a little worried about what might follow. He could not spout flames again until he dried out, and a lot could go on in the meantime. Already his opponents were huddling together. "No doubt planning some new attack," he thought. "It would be better if I found a quick dinner and then reported this incident to the others."

The dragon glided away.

"He's retreating!" cheered Jamie.

"We'd better follow him," said Edward. "He may be connected with the funny effects on our spells."

"I'd follow him anyway," said Jennifer.

Normally, a flying dragon would have outdistanced them, but Quickblast was rather shaken up, and he glided along with soft easy strokes of his tremendous wings. He did not consider being followed; nobody ever follows dragons, it's too unhealthy a prospect. The

Wynds, though, were ignorant of this tradition, and so the pursuit was joined.

Having stolen the first cow (the unfortunate Martha) so easily, Quickblast returned to the same place—Charlie Fisher's farm—for another meal. He flew low over the fields, causing barely a ripple in the grasses below. Ahead, the cows rested peacefully, lolling in the newly dampened meadow, chewing their respective cuds, thinking cow thoughts, or whatever.

Quickblast's appearance changed the bucolic scene. The cows milled about madly, shuttling first in one direction and then abruptly in another, desperately trying to evade the dragon's grasp. Had Quickblast managed his job quickly, the children would have arrived too late; but he enjoyed the cows' discomfiture and took his time looking over the menu.

After weighing several possibilities, Quickblast extended his claws and made to swoop down on a defenseless victim. Made to—tried to—but didn't. For every time he swooped, a gust of wind billowed under his wings, forcing him upward. At first, he thought it an unlucky coincidence, but after the third attempt, he suspected otherwise. Searching the landscape, he spotted four figures gesturing at him from under a grove of trees; the same four, Quick-blast assumed, he had faced earlier. At once he felt a great desire to reduce them to a pile of cinders. Alas, all he could manage was a puff of steam.

Still, the dragon formed a plan. Soaring aloft, Quickblast vanished into the clouds.

"Where'd he go?" asked Jamie.

"Up in the clouds," said Jennifer.

"I can see that, dummy. I mean where did he go from there?"

"I don't know," Edward murmured, "and I don't like it."

Alison shuddered. "Something's going to happen," she said, "and these trees block our view of the sky. Let's move out into the open."

The others agreed.

No sooner had they reached the road than the grove was caught in a raging storm. Whole trees were uprooted and sent crashing into each other, exploding in a shower of splinters and leaves. Branches, ripped from their trunks, were hurled to the ground in crackling heaps. The destruction was both awful and terribly swift, and Quickblast was immensely pleased by it. He had silently descended from directly above, lashing into the grove and destroying it with the intent of burying his adversaries beneath the wreckage.

"The sneak!" cried Jamie. "Where's his sense of honor? Of chivalry?"

"I'll teach him a lesson," said Jennifer.

"Wait," said Edward. "Let's do this together. I have an idea . . ."

If Quickblast was disappointed by anything, it was the lack of anguished cries that he had expected to hear from below. He had relished the thought of them—deliciously excruciating moans of pain and agony. But none were forthcoming.

He was about to investigate further when a wooden splinter lodged in his side. Before he could remove it, another one pierced his leg, followed by a regular volley of branches, twigs, and roots, all blazing at the point (an added touch of Jennifer's) and unerringly reaching their target.

Quickblast snarled in pain, realizing somewhat belatedly that his plan had failed. Rising from the remains of the grove, the battered dragon winged slowly off over the field, dinner forgotten as he retreated to safety.

The children trailed behind.

EIGHT

WHEN PERRY AWOKE, he found himself in the dark; not the dark of night, but an unrelenting blackness. He reached out blindly, his fingers scraping against cold, damp stone. The air was damp, too, with an earthy smell that tickled his nose.

Cautiously, Perry crawled forward, backward, and to each side, but not too far in any direction. There was a sheer wall of rock behind him, and a sheer drop everywhere else. Apparently he was meant to stay put.

Perry turned his thoughts to the dragon. Having expected pirates, the dragon had come as something of a shock, though Perry knew dragons are second to none in their love of treasure. (Of course, considering the absence of a ship, a dragon made more sense than a pirate.) And while a dragon was not a disappointment exactly, it still took some getting used to.

Perry had little time to adjust before a dull thud echoed around him. Then several blasts of fire lighted torches in the walls. In the brightening glow, Perry made out his position. He was sitting on a ledge about twenty feet from the floor of a huge cavern. To the left and right were tunnels, and from one of them a dragon had just emerged. He was lighting the torches. It was not comforting to note that this dragon was even bigger than Shimmerscale.

The dragon lumbered over to Perry. The height of the ledge allowed them to face each other head-on, a social advantage perhaps, but not one that made Perry feel more at ease.

The dragon watched him narrowly. "So, you're finally awake," he remarked. "Sleep well?"

Perry said nothing.

"Come now," prompted the dragon. "You've put out a fire and resisted a mind probe. Surely such an accomplished sorcerer's apprentice can muster a few words. For example, I'd like to know your master's name. The most foolish apprentice could tell me that."

Perry wasn't foolish, but he wasn't anyone's apprentice either. "I think you've made a mistake," he said.

"A stubborn apprentice to be sure," snarled the dragon. "And not large enough to make a satisfactory meal. A pity. I will have to consult the others about what should be done with you."

Perry turned a shade paler. "Are there more of you?" he asked.

Unwittingly, Perry had touched on a likely subject. Dragons love to talk about themselves, especially things they're proud of.

"Five of us, I'm pleased to say," the dragon answered, looking very pleased indeed. "A full Dragon Circle."

"Oh," said Perry. "That's quite a few."

The dragon nodded. "I don't wonder you're impressed," he said. "Our names alone set knights quaking in their armor."

"And your name must be the most feared of all," said Perry brightly.

"You're a smart apprentice, I'll say that for you. The name Brightfire sends a chill through the happiest gatherings."

"Well, Brightfire, sir, an important dragon like yourself must have better things to do than talk with me. My name wouldn't raise a goosepimple. Honest. So couldn't I just go home?"

Brightfire laughed. "You amuse me, boy, but

I can't grant your request. If we released you, undoubtedly you would report us to your master, and we are not yet ready to make our presence known, particularly to a sorcerer."

"Could you at least explain what you're doing here?" Perry asked. "I'm a bit confused."

"It's all perfectly straightforward," said Brightfire.

Not to Perry it wasn't. "I'd really appreciate hearing the story," he said earnestly. "I don't get much chance to speak with dragons."

"A defect in your education," snorted Brightfire. "Very well, then, I'll tell you briefly. For centuries upon centuries, we dragons roamed the length of Britain, unchallenged in our authority and power. We pillaged castles on a whim and burned villages when it tickled our fancy."

"What did you eat?" asked Perry.

"You might say we lived off the land, usually devouring flocks of sheep, or even their shepherds when we were lucky enough to find them. You've heard of shepherd's pie?"

"Oh, yes."

"The original recipe was ours. Of course, every Circle had its own variations."

"Of course," Perry repeated, suppressing a

shudder. The conversation had taken a depressing turn. "Well, if you liked Britain so much," he said, "what are you doing here?"

Brightfire snorted again, sending a sheet of flames cascading down the side of the ledge. "We were plagued by misfortune. It began when an old dragon, barely able to walk, was slain by a fellow named George. Can you imagine a dragon slain by a George? Seems impossible, doesn't it; but it happened. If I had ever met this George, the outcome would have been very different."

"No doubt," said Perry, thinking it best to be agreeable.

The memory visibly angered Brightfire. "Before long," he spat, "George's story became a legend, dealing our reputations a grievous blow. Still, we would have managed, if it hadn't been for that dratted meddler, Merlin."

"Merlin!" exclaimed Perry.

"Heard of him, eh?" Brightfire grumbled. "I'm not surprised. He was always a busybody, sticking his long nose into other people's affairs, whether they asked him to or not. Worse yet, he meddled with the kingship, watching over young Arthur, foiling our attempts to kidnap him."

"Kidnap him!" said Perry. "You mean you knew about the sword and the stone?"

Brightfire tossed his head. "There were prophesies—there usually are—and what with Merlin hovering over the lad like a mother hen, we figured out the rest. The real disaster came later, when the two of them organized the Knights of the Round Table. It was then that challenging dragons became a popular sport, not so much because of the burning, the pillaging, or even the loss of shepherds, but mostly in answer to our kidnapping of fair damsels."

"I see," said Perry, still sorrier for the shepherds than for any fair damsel.

Brightfire nodded. "It was our downfall," he admitted; "but fair damsels are hard to resist."

Perry couldn't follow him there. No matter how fancy the name, a fair damsel was always a girl. And Perry resisted girls with ease.

"Soon, the knights in their finery were scouring the countryside, challenging us to battle in pretty phrases." Brightfire smiled. "We dealt with many of them very prettily indeed."

"But surely not all," said Perry.

"No, not all," he replied, the smile fading. "The brave ones were troublesome, though they looked just like the others. Had Merlin not countered our spells, we would have survived. But he interfered as usual, and so, one Circle after another was broken. Very soon, only a few of us would have remained, to hide forever in forgotten mountain lairs.

"As yet, though, my Circle was unharmed. We met in council and decided to leave Britain until the situation improved."

"Leave?!"

"Certainly," said Brightfire. "There was no point in being foolish. Merlin was already an old man, good for another couple of centuries at best, and Arthur would be gone long before that. After their deaths, we planned to return. In the meantime, we needed a place to wait things out. There were tales among our elders of much land westward, over the sea. Dragons are not fond of the sea, or water in general, but we undertook the trip nonetheless. For days and days we flew without sighting land. Finally, we reached something shaped like a shepherd's crook."

"Cape Cod!" said Perry. "We go there in the summer."

"Hummph!" snorted Brightfire. "Very poor land for dragons, mostly sand and scrubby pine. The mountains here were better. These caverns suited our purposes admirably. So we settled down, sealed ourselves in, and went to sleep."

"Till when?" Perry asked.

"Three days ago."

"Impossible," said Perry. "That would mean you slept for hundreds and hundreds of years."

"Did we?" said Brightfire, flicking his tail. "How interesting."

"It's more than that," said Perry. "How could you sleep for so long?"

"Oh, that's easy. When you live for thousands of years, a few centuries of sleep one way or the other don't really matter. Besides, we were tired."

Perry shook his head. "I don't understand the sleeping part," he said, "but the rest of it seems pretty clear. You fled from your enemies in England, sort of like the pilgrims."

Brightfire looked puzzled. "Pilgrims?" he repeated, rolling the word around in his mouth. "What are pilgrims? They sound tasty."

"You're getting the wrong idea," said Perry. "The pilgrims were the first settlers here. And like you, they were forced to leave England. Over three hundred years ago."

"Three hundred years, you say," mused Brightfire with a gleam in his eye. "Then there must be a lot of villages nearby."

He didn't seem to be getting the message. "You'll burn no villages here!" Perry shouted defiantly, hoping a brave knight would have said the same.

"Oh, won't we?" Brightfire hissed wickedly. "And who is there to stop us?"

Before Perry could reply, Quickblast shuffled into the cavern followed by three other dragons. One of them was Shimmerscale.

"What happened to you?" Brightfire demanded. "You look like some kind of porcupine. And where is dinner." His tone was that of a disturbed and hungry dragon. Not a tone to be trifled with.

Quickblast pulled a few more sticks from his side. "I was attacked," he said, with a trace of discomfort.

Had Brightfire an eyebrow, he would have arched it. "By whom?" he asked skeptically.

In all honesty, Quickblast wasn't sure. "It may have been four wizards," he said. "I came back to warn you."

Perry smiled. He thought he knew who was responsible.

"Four wizards!" roared Brightfire. "Four wizards have not assembled together since the ancient wars on Salisbury Plain. It's hardly likely now."

Quickblast stared at his clawed feet. "Well, it was difficult to see in the twilight."

"Whoever they were," said Brightfire, "we can deal with them later. I trust you didn't lead them back here."

"They won't find us," said Quickblast. "I hid the tunnel entrance with a spell."

"Good," said Greatwing, an older dragon whose evil deeds would make a tale by themselves. "We have other business to consider at present."

"What business is that?" asked Perry.

"No concern of yours," hissed Greatwing. "If I had had my way, you'd be done to a turn by now."

"But my way still rules," said Brightfire, "and I think he may be of use to us. So let's get on with our little problem."

The dragons moved to the far side of the cavern, leaving Perry to his own thoughts about the possible variations of shepherd's pie.

NINE

THE MOUTH of the narrow valley, its steep sides and ragged boulders sharply outlined in the moonlight, was a forbidding place. A quiet one, too, until footsteps broke the early evening silence.

"I'm pooped," said Jamie, wiping his forehead wearily.

"Well, kindly unpoop yourself," said Jennifer. "We've got to find that dragon, and I know he landed around here somewhere."

"Not much room for a dragon to hide," noted Alison.

"What should we do?" asked Jamie.

"Go get Father," said Edward. "He knows more about dragons than we do. Besides, he . . . Jennifer, what are you doing now?"

"Just looking." Jennifer was sure the dragon had come down nearby, and she was not about to give up, at least not until every inch of the valley had been searched for clues. She sloshed through the puddles left by the rain, blazing a trail of soggy footprints.

"Aha!" she cried suddenly.

"What is it?" asked Jamie.

"Come and see for yourself," she replied, kneeling by the imprint of a large clawmark.

They did so.

"Tracks!" Jamie exclaimed.

"They lead to the base of this cliff," said Jennifer.

"I guess the dragon came down and then took off again," said Alison.

Jennifer shook her head. "He came down and stayed down," she insisted. "I know it."

"Now really," said Edward, "how can you *know* it?"

Jamie sighed, foreseeing a long debate. He leaned contentedly against the cliff.

Jennifer gasped suddenly.

"Jamie vanished inside the cliff!" cried Alison.

Jamie picked himself up off the ground. "What are you babbling about?" he asked. "I just slipped, I think, and . . ." Jamie looked around in surprise at the cave that had mysteriously appeared around him. "Where did this come from? Alison, why are you looking at me like that?"

"She's not looking at you," said Edward. "That's the problem. She can't see you. Neither can I. We can only hear your voice through the wall of the cliff."

"What wall? What cliff?" asked Jamie. "I can see you perfectly well."

Edward reached out to touch the controversial cliff. His hand should have pressed up against the rocks and dirt his eyes told him were there, but instead his arm simply disappeared up to his elbow. "Jamie, do you see my whole arm?" he asked.

"Of course."

Edward turned to his sisters. "The cliff must be an illusion," he said. "It's like a one-way mirror: we can't see in, but anyone inside can see out. And there's nothing solid there at all."

"Are you sure?" asked Alison.

"Watch this," said Edward, stepping into, and then through the imaginary cliff.

Jamie grinned at him.

Edward looked around slowly. "Amazing," he murmured, examining the sides of the cave. "A first-rate enchantment." He glanced back outside. "Come on in, girls."

Jennifer and Alison shrugged their shoulders,

took a deep breath, and plunged through.

Jennifer whistled in awe. "Quite a trick," she marveled. "Indeed it is," agreed Edward. "A good thing you noticed those clawmarks, Jenny. We never would have found this otherwise."

"What about my part?" asked Jamie.

Edward smiled. "Your credit goes to your tired feet."

"Speaking of feet," said Alison, "those clawmarks lead into the darkness. It looks like a long deep tunnel."

"Then let's not waste any more time," said Jennifer. "Let's explore it."

They slowly groped their way forward along the cold stone walls, stumbling over the loose stones and dips in the tunnel floor. In the darkness, they blindly followed the right-hand passage of a fork. The passage sloped gently downward, leading them further and further underground.

"I think there's a light up ahead," whispered Alison, halting abruptly.

Silently, they all crept closer. The light brightened before them, revealing a large cavern. They peered into it on their hands and knees. Edward pointed to a circle of five dragons, who were chanting in unison. Every few seconds, a flash of light rose from their midst and burst against the cavern roof.

"Look, there's Perry," said Alison softly. "Over on that raised ledge."

"Can we attract his attention?" asked Jamie.

"Not without attracting... Look out! Duck!" hissed Edward.

Brightfire lifted his head, sniffing deeply of the cavern air. "The smell of humans is strong for just one small boy," he said.

"Nervous, eh?" chided Greatwing, who disliked interrupting a spell in progress.

"Certainly not."

"Then let's finish the enchantment. Maybe this one will work."

"Perhaps finishing it near the rest of the treasure would help," suggested Quickblast. "We've tried everything else."

"Possibly," mused Brightfire.

Shimmerscale scowled. "What about the boy?" he asked.

"He's not going anywhere."

"But a sorcerer's apprentice . . ."

"All right," said Brightfire, "we'll leave Shortflight to keep watch."

Shortflight was the scrawniest of the five

dragons, not a likely member of the Circle except for one redeeming feature: he thought Brightfire the smartest, bravest, most wonderful dragon that ever lived. And Brightfire liked his taste.

"Will they come this way?" asked Jennifer.

"No," said Edward, "they're going out that other tunnel."

As the dragons filed out, Shortflight waddled over to the base of Perry's ledge and sat down.

"It's only one dragon against the four of us," said Jennifer. "We managed one before."

"No good," said Edward. "We don't know how far the others are going. At the first sound of trouble, they may return. And how can we defeat even a small dragon silently?"

"Oh, I don't know," said Alison mischievously, "maybe we could put him to sleep."

Edward looked doubtful. "I know it's your specialty, Alison," he said. "And we all could help. But don't forget, this is a dragon we're talking about."

"As you said, though," added Jennifer, "a small dragon."

"There's no such thing as a *small* dragon," said Jamie. "Some are just bigger than others."

"What can we lose?" asked Alison.

Edward sighed. "All right," he said, "let's try it."

Shortflight was standing resolutely at attention, very pleased to be on guard. He yearned for the chance to prove himself a fierce dragon—he yearned for this often—but on this job it now seemed the more he yearned, the sleepier he got. Shortflight blinked repeatedly at the walls and settled to the floor; just to be a bit more comfortable, he told himself. Before long, he was stretched out flat on his stomach. (Dragons cannot sleep on their backs, of course, because of the spikes.)

"If I had a hat, Alison, I would doff it to you," said Edward. "Let's hope he isn't a light sleeper."

"I hope Perry is," muttered Jennifer. "That dummy has fallen asleep, too." It wasn't really Perry's fault, however; some of the spell had crept up to his ledge.

Stealthily, they stole across the cavern, stopping suddenly when Shortflight began to snore, exhaling flames in periodic bursts. With careful timing, they dashed past him safely, all except Jamie, who was singed on the seat of his pants.

"How will we get him down?" asked Alison.

"Float him," said Edward. "The four of us

should be able to manage it."

"Perry!" Jamie called out in a stage whisper.

"Hmmmmmmm."

"Wake up, you idiot," growled Jennifer. "We're here to rescue you."

Perry yawned sleepily. "Who's we?" he asked.

"Don't be dense!"

Perry came abruptly awake. What he thought was a dream sounded too much like the real Jennifer. He rubbed his eyes and looked down.

"We'll float you to the floor, Perry," whispered Edward. "All right?"

He nodded.

"Whenever you're ready."

Perry stepped off the ledge and slowly descended in an upright position, like a helium balloon a few days after a parade.

"How did you find me?" Perry gasped.

"Later, Perry," said Edward. "Let's get out of here first."

They hurried back toward the tunnel, stopping short when a wall of fire blazed up before them.

"One move," snarled Brightfire ominously from behind them, "just one move, and I'll fry the lot of you."

TEN

BRIGHTFIRE subjected each of the children to his terrifying gaze. It was very unpleasant to stand quietly while the dragon made his inspection, but the thought of being fried was even more unpleasant. So nobody moved.

"Here, no doubt, we have some noble rescuers," said Brightfire. "More apprentices, perhaps?"

"Who's an apprentice?" whispered Jennifer.

"He thinks I am," said Perry. "And he must think—"

"Shortflight!" roared Brightfire, cutting off any further explanation.

The sleepy dragon jerked to his feet. "Yes, Brightfire?" he said meekly.

"We have some new visitors." He turned back to the children. "I know Shortflight didn't fall asleep without help. Which one of you did

78

it? Or was it a combined effort? Come now, this is not the time for modesty."

Maybe not, but all the same no one stepped forward.

"Honestly, Brightfire," said Shortflight. "I don't understand—"

"Quiet! I'll explain it to you later."

"What's happened here?" asked Greatwing, as he and the other dragons reentered the cavern. "We were wondering what delayed you, Brightfire."

"I've been welcoming some new guests. As I said before, Greatwing, the smell of humans was strong for just one small boy. I suspected there were others, which is why I left you to check on Shortflight. And look what I found—a whole family. Don't try to deny it, the resemblance is quite plain." He stared intently at Jennifer. "In fact, you even look familiar to me."

"But how did they find us?" asked Shortflight.

"An interesting question. Well, Quickblast?!" Brightfire snapped. "How did they? Are these your four wizards? A handful of children?"

Understandably, Quickblast looked a little

embarrassed. "I couldn't see them clearly," he mumbled.

"No doubt," said Brightfire. "But how does that explain your failure to defeat mere children?"

Quickblast stared in dismay at the floor.

"What shall we do with them?" asked Shimmerscale.

"Since we missed dinner," said Greatwing, "perhaps . . ."

Brightfire shook his head. "They're too stringy," he said. "Except for this one," he added, prodding Jamie with a claw.

"Leave him alone!" Jennifer demanded.

It was a dangerous thing to say. But, instead of lashing Jennifer with his tail or reducing her to ashes with a burst of his fiery breath or any one of a hundred other unfortunate possibilities, Brightfire simply stared at her.

"That face," he murmured. "That look of determination . . . I know why you look so familiar. You were at the summoning two nights ago." He glanced around. "And the others, too." Brightfire turned to his Circle. "You remember that spell that called to us. I answered it, but was cut off before clearly establishing contact."

"If they're capable of a summoning, even a clumsy one, they may be useful," mused Shimmerscale.

"Possibly," said Brightfire.

The idea came as a big surprise to the children.

"Whatever it is, we won't do it!" Perry shouted. "Not after what you did to those poor shepherds. You'd better let us go, or our father will take care of you."

Brightfire cast Perry a searing look. "Father!" he exclaimed. "Of course, I should have thought of it before. Such children must have a very skilled father. He must be a sorcerer or wizard himself."

"No," said Perry, "he's a professor."

"Silence!" cried Brightfire. "An interesting development, this father."

"He'll never help you," said Jamie.

"Oh, you're wrong there," said Brightfire. "I'm sure he cares deeply about his children. Wouldn't want anything unhealthy to happen to them. No, he will help us, and thanks to your summoning, we know where to find him. How ironic."

That last remark showed the dragon's true colors—dreadful is too kind a word for him.

"Why do you want Father, anyway?" asked Alison curiously.

"I suppose I can tell you," said Brightfire. "We need him to recover our treasure."

Perry looked puzzled. "But you have tons of the stuff," he declared.

Brightfire waved his comment aside. "Mere baubles," he said bitterly. "Impressive in their bulk, I suppose, but no more than that. The finer, more exquisite things are at the bottom of a mountain lake."

"How did they get there?" asked Jennifer.

"It was my doing," Quickblast admitted. "The wind suddenly shifted under me on our arrival, and I dropped the chests in the water."

"Couldn't you recover them?" asked Jamie.

"We've been trying," said Brightfire. "It's no use. Our spells have no power over water. Hence the need for your father. Greatwing!"

"Yes, Brightfire?"

"You will go fetch their father. I will give you directions. Take care to avoid detection. There shouldn't be any trouble once you explain the situation. But even if there is, I want him alive. Understand?"

"Of course."

"Good. Now, children, since we don't want

your father to be distracted, you will remain in the treasure cave until this business is settled. Shimmerscale will escort you and stay to see that you don't get lonely."

"Come along," ordered Shimmerscale.

"You can't do this," said Jamie. "It's inhuman."

"Quite," agreed the dragon. "How nice of you to mention it."

PROFESSOR WYND stood before the kitchen stove, impatiently shifting his weight from one foot to the other. Occasionally, he stirred a simmering pot of stew; his thoughts, though, were focused on blossoming apple trees and unruly porcelain gargoyles. And unlike the tranquil stew, his thoughts were bubbling furiously.

Unfortunately, all that bubbling hadn't been much help. The Professor knew a powerful being, when conjuring spells, could disrupt nearby enchantments, but he also knew that dozens of beings were capable of such disruptions.

His fingers drummed on the countertop, the only sound in the kitchen. Or the house for that matter. This was unusual; at dinnertime, the kitchen invariably held at least one of his brood wailing like a starving vulture. And yet the Professor was alone. "Come to think of it," he said to himself, "I haven't seen any of the children for hours. I guess they'll show up when they get hungry enough."

Suddenly, the vibrations from a tremendous thump shook the house. Some of the stew sloshed onto the stove, and a pitcher fell off the counter, shattering on the floor. Professor Wynd dropped his ladle and rushed outside to investigate.

Greatwing stood on the front lawn, checking himself for bruises. But his rocky landing had only damaged his pride. Once a most accomplished flyer, especially famous for his wingtip roll, he was now a little rusty.

At the sight of the dragon, the Professor halted abruptly. It wasn't so much surprise that held him, as the force of the dragon's ancient bearing and the malevolent look in his eyes.

"Good evening," said the Professor politely. Well-versed in dragon lore, he knew of their fondness for courtesies.

Greatwing looked up. "So it is," he said. "Very pleasant after the rain."

"May I ask what prompts your visit?" the

Professor continued in the same polite tone.

The dragon smiled wickedly. "You may indeed," he said. "I'm looking for the father of three boys and two girls. Perhaps you can help me."

The Professor looked startled. "I have five children fitting your description," he said slowly.

"And do they have a magical disposition?"

"You could put it that way."

"I did," said Greatwing testily. His landing had shortened his temper. "If you care for your children's welfare, you will come with me."

"If any harm has—"

"Save your threats," interrupted the dragon. "You're in no position to make them. Shall we go?"

"It would seem I must."

"A wise conclusion. Now climb up on my back and hold on tightly. If you fall off, I'll have to catch you as best I can."

The Professor took a secure grip.

"AH, THEY RETURN," said Brightfire. "Any problems?"

"He has been most cooperative," said Greatwing.

Brightfire nodded. "Excellent," he said. "Well, fellow, you have been granted the singular honor of aiding a Dragon Circle."

"I'm deeply moved."

Brightfire watched him warily. "So I see. But I'm forgetting my manners. We haven't made the proper introductions. I am Brightfire. You've already met Greatwing. On my left is Quickblast, on my right, Shortflight. The other member of our Circle, Shimmerscale, is keeping your children company in a safe place. Now you have us at an advantage. Might we have the pleasure of your name?"

"Alexander Wynd."

The dragons snorted in rage.

"You bear an ancient name, Wynd," said Brightfire sternly. "Many of our kind fell at the hand of your forebears."

"Many, but not all."

"True enough," returned Brightfire sharply, "yet their vigilance was a constant irritation. How appropriate that you should have the opportunity to make amends."

"Isn't it though."

"Your tone is less than friendly," Brightfire noted. "No doubt you are worried about your children."

"How are they?"

"Very well, for the moment. And they will remain so if you'll help us."

"Help you with what?"

"A part of our treasure lies at the bottom of a mountain lake. We want you to raise it."

The Professor nodded.

"I see," he said.

"I hope you do," Brightfire said earnestly. "They are such talented children. It would be a pity . . ."

"And if I raise the treasure?"

"Then you all go free. You have my word."

This was small comfort to the Professor, who understood that in these matters a dragon's word was a fragile thing. "I'd like to see the children first," he said.

Brightfire shook his head. "I'm afraid that's not possible. We've already had a sampling of what they can do on their own. If you were to join them, there might be some foolish attempt at escape. I wouldn't put it past a family of Wynds. And we don't want any trouble; you might get hurt."

The Professor considered pressing the point, but decided it would be useless. He really had no choice. "Very well," he said.

"A sensible approach," said Brightfire. "Let us hope it stays that way."

ELEVEN

THE SIGHT of the treasure made a big impression on everyone, even Perry, who had already seen it twice. But treasure is like that, which may partly explain why dragons are so fond of it.

"Look at all this stuff!" exclaimed Jennifer. "Why, there's enough here for ten kings."

"Ten!" snarled Shimmerscale. "What do you mean, ten? Twenty would be closer to the mark. Twenty-three to be exact. I kept track."

"How did you do that?" asked Jamie.

Shimmerscale's tongue licked the edge of his snout. "How do you think?"

Jamie dropped the subject.

"But why do you have two different caves?" asked Alison quickly. "Seems like a lot of bother."

"Tradition," said Shimmerscale. "The treasure is stored apart as a token of our esteem."

"Do all dragons have so much of it?" Edward asked.

"We have done particularly well," Shimmerscale boasted proudly. "Of course, the sunken chests hold even more spectacular things."

"What have we here?" asked Jamie, picking up a bookbag. "Kind of odd-looking treasure."

"Very funny," said Perry. "It's mine, dummy. I must have dropped it when . . . well, before."

"Wow!" cried Alison, hefting a jewel-encrusted broadsword. "This thing weighs a ton."

"Chiefly ceremonial," Shimmerscale explained. "The jewels are awkward in a fight, at least they were for the former owner."

"Oh," said Alison, letting it fall abruptly.

"Just what you need for your play, Perry," said Jennifer. "That sword would be a lot better than the piece of junk you're using now."

Perry frowned. "What do you mean, junk?" he challenged. "There's nothing the matter with my sword. It's the scourge of—"

"The what?" asked Jennifer.

"Scourge," he repeated. "S-C-O-U-R-G-E. If you don't know what it means, look it up. As I was saying, the scourge of goblins, giants, dragons—"

"Here now," said Shimmerscale, "no more of that kind of talk."

"Be serious, Perry," said Jamie. "Your sword isn't in the same class with any of these."

"It is so," said Perry. "King Arthur would never have had less than a truly superior sword."

"Lucky you don't have to prove it," taunted Jennifer. "I'll bet we wouldn't even notice your sword among all the splendid ones here."

"Is that so?!" said Perry angrily. "Well, I'll show you. I have it right here in my bookbag." Striding forward resolutely, he repeated his favorite line from the play.

"With my trusty sword, Excalibur, I shall rout the dragons from our midst!" he cried, unsheathing Excalibur with a flourish.

At the mention of dragons, Shimmerscale started to interrupt again, but the words stuck in his throat. For once more, as Perry said that line, the sword burst into flames. To Shimmerscale's eyes, Perry truly held the scourge of dragons in ancient times—King Arthur's dreaded sword, Excalibur. And though Perry was not the image of King Arthur, Shimmerscale was terrified nonetheless.

Perry and the others stared in awe at the flaming sword. No spell of theirs had wrought the transformation. But magic answers to its own rules, and somehow Perry's line, with actual dragons nearby, had triggered the sword's symbolic identity, releasing a powerful enchantment.

Whatever the reason, Perry couldn't have been more pleased. He pressed his advantage. "You will do our bidding," he said, brandishing the sword at the hapless dragon, "or I will deal with you as you so justly deserve." (It was another line from the play.)

Shimmerscale could have burned Perry to a crisp, but he was too flustered by the sight of Excalibur. The possibility of becoming a crisp never occurred to Perry. As he approached, the cowering dragon turned and bolted from the cavern.

Once he reached the open air, Shimmerscale paused. "That was close," he muttered. "I must inform the Circle. It will take us all to battle Excalibur." But a dragon would sooner die than leave his treasure unprotected; so, as Shimmerscale rose from the ground, his tail lashed out. Several boulders were knocked into the tunnel entrance, sealing it off.

The dragon's hasty exit caught the children by surprise.

"Come on," said Edward, rousing the others. "We've got to escape." But before anyone had moved, clouds of dust billowed into the cavern.

"What happened?" asked Jennifer, wiping the dirt from her face.

"I don't know," said Jamie, "but at least we weren't fried."

"Not yet, anyway," said Alison.

Perry was staring at his sword, which had resumed its normal appearance. "Oh well," he said, "it was nice while it lasted."

Edward pulled down a torch from the wall. "Alison, Jennifer, take the other two torches," he said. "Then we'll see what's out there."

They reached the prong of the fork successfully, but just beyond that, the tunnel was filled in.

"Now what?" asked Perry.

"With enough spells," said Alison, "we could probably shift these rocks eventually. But it would take hours, and the dragons would return before we escaped."

"Well," said Edward, "the only other place we can go is the main cavern."

"Maybe there's an exit from there," said Jennifer hopefully.

"The dragons certainly don't have one," said Jamie. "There are two tunnels leading out of that cavern. One goes up here, the other goes to the treasure."

"Let's check it, anyway," said Edward. "Perhaps we'll find something to help us."

With Edward and Alison in front, they made their way to the main cavern.

"Hellooo!" cried Perry.

"Hellooo!" echoed the cavern.

"Be quiet, Perry," said Jennifer. "We're trying to think."

"You'll need more than quiet for that."

"Spread out, everyone," instructed Alison. "Look for a hole or a crack or something."

Perry wandered over near the ledge where he had been held prisoner. There were no holes or cracks to be seen.

"Nothing here!" called out Jamie from another wall.

To Perry's left was a column of rock, half-hidden in the shadows. Perry poked his head behind it.

"Hey!" he shouted. "I've found a big crack."

The others ran to his side.

"So you have," said Alison. "A good-sized crevice. I wonder if the dragons ever noticed it?"

"They probably thought it was too small to bother about," said Jamie.

"Well, it's not too small for us," said Jennifer. "And wherever it leads will be better than waiting here."

There was no argument about that.

"What about the treasure?" asked Perry.

"Worrying about treasure is the least of our problems," said Alison. "Let's get going." She ducked through the crevice, and the rest followed.

"Pretty dusty in here," said Jennifer.

Alison knelt and scooped up a handful of dust. "It's like silt," she said.

"Silt?" Perry repeated.

"The fine sand at a bottom of a riverbed," she told him.

Jamie thrust a torch into the darkness. He had taken it from the main cavern. "It's all caved in here to the left," he said.

"That simplifies matters," said Alison. "Off to the right we go."

They traveled in silence until Edward observed that the passage was shrinking.

"I already bumped my head," said Alison. "I was hoping it didn't mean anything."

It did. Soon, everyone was crouching but Perry.

"I'm getting a permanent stoop," moaned Jennifer.

"Think positive," advised Edward. "The dragons can't follow us here."

"Lucky them," gasped Jamie.

The tunnel finally emptied into another cavern. While the others stretched their backs, Perry examined a pile of rocks heaped against one wall. "Maybe they block a hole," he said, flinging a few of them aside.

"What are you doing, Perry?" asked Jennifer.

"Trying to rescue us. But I can't do it alone."

"Nice to hear you admit it," she replied, as she and Jamie joined him.

"Come on, Alison," said Edward.

Alison frowned. "I don't like it," she muttered. "We should be more careful . . ."

Meanwhile, Jamie and Jennifer struggled with a huge boulder that refused to budge. Perry began pushing away some of the smaller rocks around it.

"I think that's enough, Perry," said Jamie. "All right, Jenny, let's try it again. One, two, three. Heave!"

The boulder shifted slightly.

"Stubborn, isn't it?" grumbled Jennifer.

"Try again," said Perry.

This time the dirt and stone packed at the front slowly gave way, sending the boulder toppling to the cavern floor.

"Hooray!" shouted the happy trio.

"Oh, no!" gasped Edward.

Where the boulder had stood, a stream of water spilled out over the rocks.

"Now we know how the silt got here," said Alison. "An underground stream once flowed through here. Probably diverted by a rock fall."

"There'll be a stream again if we don't do something about it," said Edward.

Despite their efforts, though, the water poured through.

"This is all my fault," Perry groaned.

"You can't have the blame to yourself," said Jennifer. "Some of it's mine."

"Mine, too," insisted Jamie.

A small pool was rapidly growing on the cavern floor.

"Argue about it later," said Alison. "Right now, let's check out the nooks and fissures here.

The flood nipping at their heels spurred them to search quickly. In the next half-hour, most of the new cavern was painstakingly examined; unfortunately, the only thing that changed was the water level. It was steadily rising.

Edward had climbed up to the higher ledges. Just above his head was a rock wedged tightly into the cavern ceiling. The rock intrigued him. Unlike the smooth surrounding stone, it was rough and dusty, jutting out from the curve of the roof like a plug in a hole. Turning to get a better view, he kicked some loose dirt and stones over the side of the ledge.

"Be careful," cautioned Alison from a lower crag. "What are you doing, anyway?"

"I'm about to experiment," Edward replied. "Watch out below."

A light flashed from his fingertips, cracking the rock's surface. Again and again the light flashed, chipping at the impassive stone. The web of cracks extended, crisscrossing the exposed point until the rock finally crumbled into several pieces and fell away.

"What did you find?" asked Alison.

Edward sighed in relief. "The moon and the stars," he said. "Or maybe they found us."

"Not a moment too soon," said Jamie. The water was lapping at his feet.

Edward poked at the hole. "It's not far to the

surface, and we can pull ourselves up on some exposed roots ."

"Jennifer! Perry!" shouted Alison. "Come quickly."

The two youngest Wynds were exploring a water fissure. "Let's go, Perry," said Jennifer impatiently. "You heard Alison, didn't you?"

"I'm coming, I'm coming," he replied. "It's slippery down here."

Jennifer helped him up. They threaded their way around the cavern, trying to avoid getting wet. One pool of water was particularly wide.

"Should we wade across?" asked Perry.

"Not me," said Jennifer. "I'm going to jump. It's not much more than a yard. I've done farther than that in school." She threw their torch to the other side and leaped after it. Her landing was bumpy. "Watch out for the sharp spots," she said, wincing.

Perry looked at the water doubtfully. The water looked back smugly. What Perry needed was a running start, but there wasn't enough room for that. Still, if Jennifer could jump, so could he. Taking a deep breath, he leaped.

And missed.

Jennifer couldn't help laughing. "Oh, Perry, you're such a dummy. You've soaked both of us. Do you . . . Perry, what's the matter? You look faint."

He really did.

"My ankle feels funny."

"Jamie! Alison!" shouted Jennifer. "Perry's been hurt."

Jamie scrambled down the rocks like a tipsy mountain goat. "What's wrong?" he asked.

"I think Perry's twisted his ankle."

"Does it hurt much, Perry?" he asked.

Perry shook his head. "Just throbs."

"Well, you shouldn't walk on a bad ankle. I'll have to carry you." He eased Perry onto his back, and with Jennifer steadying him, they climbed to the base of Edward's ledge. Alison was already halfway up, waiting to help the others. Jamie and Jennifer hoisted Perry to a narrow seat of rock, and after lengthy repetitions of hoisting and climbing, everyone finally reached the top.

Because of the roots, scrambling through the hole was easy, but dirty. Perry had the most trouble, managing awkwardly with only one good leg.

The sky looked especially beautiful to all of them that night. The air was clear, and the clouds had blown away, leaving the moon and the stars shining brightly in their proper places.

"Why, look!" Jennifer exclaimed. "There's the lake."

"But what's that?" asked Jamie, pointing to a light blazing just beyond it.

"I don't know," said Edward. "Campfire, maybe."

"It could be a signal from Father," said Perry.

"Or the dragons," Jamie added.

"Either way," said Jennifer, "we should investigate."

"Wait a minute," said Alison. "How's your ankle, Perry?"

"Not too bad. It hurts a little when I put my weight on it."

Alison nodded. "First, we'll make you a crutch. Then we'll check out the lake."

Five minutes later, they were on their way.

TWELVE

NEAR THE SHORE of the lake lay a small glade guarded by a ring of fir trees. The place was a favorite picnic ground and campsite—for people, that is—but never before in its long history, had the glade played host to dragons.

In the middle of the glade a bright fire was set to blazing as soon as the dragons arrived: not the ordinary red and orange kind, but a pure white one, rimmed with blue. Then Professor Wynd stood before it and softly began to chant a string of spells. The dragons watched him closely.

"Isn't he ready yet?" asked Quickblast nervously, when only a few minutes had passed.

Dragons don't often ask such questions. They are familiar with almost all forms of magic; water magic is the big exception. Dragons cannot work it (fire and water don't mix), and being lazy creatures, they have never concerned themselves with understanding its spells.

"Wynd!" snapped Brightfire. He, too, felt uneasy.

The Professor turned from the fire. "Yes?"

"How long must we wait here? Are you making progress?"

"It will take time," the Professor answered, "even longer with interruptions. The treasure lies deep, and the spells are complicated."

Something in the Professor's tone troubled Greatwing. "Would you attempt to deceive us?" he asked.

"Deceive a Dragon Circle? It has never been done."

"True enough, Greatwing," said Brightfire impatiently. "Wynd, return to your spells."

All heads suddenly turned at a rustling from above. With an unceremonious bump, Shimmerscale landed behind them.

"What are you doing here?" Brightfire snarled.

Shimmerscale gasped. "I've come to warn you!" he cried.

"Warn us?" Shortflight repeated. He glanced around. "About what?"

"Excalibur. That sorcerer's apprentice, the

young one, brandished it at me in the treasure cavern."

"You're talking nonsense," sneered Greatwing. "That sword is not in our collection. We could not abide it."

"I know it isn't in our collection," said Shimmerscale. "The apprentice had it with him."

"Tell us what happened," Brightfire ordered.

"All of them were admiring our treasure. Then the younger girl began taunting the apprentice about his sword. Apparently it was in the canvas bag he dropped when I first found him."

"You never mentioned any canvas bag before," said Quickblast.

"I didn't think it was important. Who would have expected such a thing? The apprentice pulled out the sword, saying something about routing dragons. It was Excalibur."

"Just like that?" asked Brightfire.

"E-exactly."

Brightfire snorted. "Bah! I'm surrounded by incompetents. First a tale of wizards, and now this. Can't anyone control these children?"

The Professor had often wondered the same thing.

"But the treasure," said Greatwing, "what about the treasure?"

"Oh," said Shimmerscale, "it's perfectly safe. I sealed off the cavern entrance."

"You're sure?"

"Absolutely. The children can never dig themselves out, though removing the boulders should be quite simple for us."

Brightfire nodded. "Good," he declared. "Then all still goes well. We can check on this so-called Excalibur later. I hope you're listening, Wynd. I know you'll agree that a sealed cavern is no place for children."

WELL OVER an hour passed. Finally, Professor Wynd stepped back from the flames. "It's ready," he said.

"About time," Greatwing grumbled.

"Begin!" commanded Brightfire.

The Professor plunged his hands into the fire. He held them there for several seconds and then removed them. His hands glowed with a white radiance.

"Excellent," said Brightfire.

Turning on his heel, the Professor walked slowly toward a tall ridge overlooking the lake. The dragons followed.

EDWARD AND JENNIFER scouted ahead while Alison and Jamie helped Perry, who was inexperienced with a crutch. It was easier for him nearer the lake, where the ground was smoother.

"Do you feel it?" Alison whispered to Jamie.

He nodded. It was as though the air itself was filled with magic.

"Look!" hissed Edward, ducking behind a rock.

Not more than two hundred yards away, Professor Wynd was leading a procession of dragons toward the lake.

"Looks like the Pied Piper," said Jennifer.

Perry nodded. "With awfully big rats."

"What's Father doing?" asked Jamie.

Edward frowned. "He's about to raise the treasure, I guess."

Perry was counting. "All five dragons are there," he said. "So they've heard about the sword."

"But they don't know we've escaped," said Jamie.

"That's our advantage," said Alison. "And we must watch carefully for the chance to use it."

The Professor climbed to the top of the ridge alone, raising his arms before him. He looked down at the lake and shouted a single word aloud. The wind gusted, stirring the placid waters, whipping them into a stormy rage. The air grew misty as white-crested waves rolled toward the beach, crashing beyond the shoreline.

"Why the storm?" asked Jennifer, her hair streaming behind her.

"Wait and see," said Edward.

The Professor's clothes flapped wildly, but he stared stonily into space, seemingly oblivious to the tempest around him. Suddenly, his hands came together in a single clap, sending a bolt like lightning to pierce the water below. A great cloud of steam rose from the surface. The water churned into a whirlpool, which, twisting slowly downward, forced a tunnel of air to the lake's bottom.

As they watched from the shore, the dragons shuffled anxiously. They could hardly conceal their impatience, and these last few minutes had seemed interminable.

The strain proved too much for the aged Greatwing. "I must see for myself," he announced abruptly, winging into the sky.

This was too much for the rest of them.

"Come," said Brightfire, spreading his wings in turn. The others followed. It made a strange picture: the five dragons hovering over the whirlpool, heedless of the surrounding storm, intent only on what lay below.

"The chests! I see them!" cried Quickblast.

Eager for a better look, the dragons craned their long necks forward, edging closer to the surface.

The Professor had waited for this moment. He spoke another word that was gathered up and lost in the storm. Then he clapped his hands again.

The walls of the watery tunnel surged up, engulfing Shortflight and Quickblast at once. Shimmerscale and Greatwing desperately beat back their wings; the water battered them relentlessly. The fire roared from their snouts but was quenched by the spray. They weakened at last, and with a cheerless cry of defeat, fell headlong into the vortex.

Only Brightfire remained. He had been farthest from the water when the trap was sprung, so he was still able to fight the whirlpool's grip. Now, his great strength enabled him to slowly escape the twisting funnel.

The children had risen and were watching all this in amazement.

"Of course!" said Edward, snapping his fingers. "Father didn't plan to help the dragons. But he needed the water to defeat them."

"Look!" exclaimed Alison. "Brightfire is escaping."

"Come on!" said Jennifer. "Father did his part. Now it's our turn."

They conferred quickly at the water's edge. Then, joining hands, they combined their strength in a single spell.

A small wave, about to break on the rocks, turned abruptly away, charging toward the whirlpool. Like a snowball rolling downhill, the wave grew and grew, a towering wall of water rushing toward the unsuspecting Brightfire.

The wave broke just behind the struggling dragon, engulfing him with such force that he too was driven into the churning waters. "Curse you, Wynd!" cried Brightfire in a last gasp. "Curse you!"

For an instant the water boiled frantically. Then a calm returned. Drenched in spray, Professor Wynd walked down wearily from the top of the ridge.

THE CHILDREN sat around their father in the living room, sipping hot chocolate. It was past midnight, but no one felt like sleeping just yet.

"What I don't understand," Jennifer was saying, "is why Perry's sword burst into flames in school and in the treasure cavern."

"Because that is what Excalibur would have done," said the Professor.

"But it wasn't really Excalibur," she insisted; "it was just a prop from a school play."

"Ah, well," the Professor continued, "that's the interesting part. You see, symbolically the sword was Excalibur and in the presence of real dragons and an ancient pledge to rout them, the sword tapped one of the wild currents of magic that wander loose in the world. And lucky for us it did."

Perry looked knowingly at Jennifer. "I told you my sword was special," he said.

"Father, how did you know the dragons would hover over the lake?" Jamie asked. "They could have waited for the spell to bring the treasure ashore."

"I didn't," he answered simply. "But I hoped they would and prepared accordingly. Dragons inspire greed in others, but only because they are consumed by it themselves. And they have a great deal of curiosity. I depended on both things."

Alison shuddered. "And still Brightfire almost got away," she said.

The Professor nodded. "True, but he was no match for the entire family."

"Just think," sighed Jamie, "of all that treasure under the lake."

"And under the mountain, too," noted Edward. "All covered by water too, now, I suppose."

"Where it shall remain," said their father. "We want no part of dragon treasure. It breeds trouble, always has. What concerns me is your ankle, Perry. Does it hurt much?"

"A little," Perry admitted.

"We'll have the doctor look at it tomorrow. You'll probably have to stay off it for a week or two."

"Hooray!" Perry shouted.

"You're taking the news surprisingly well," said Alison. "It may cost you your part in the play."

"Oh, that's all right. I've got a what-do-you-call-it?"

"Understudy?" suggested Edward.

"Right."

"But you'll have to give up being King Arthur," said Jamie.

"And that means giving up Queen Guinevere, too," Edward reminded him.

"I know." Perry sighed happily. "I know."